HOW KAMASUTRA CHANGED THE WORLD

SAM RAMSEY

Made with ♥ on the Notion Press Platform
www.notionpress.com

Contents

INTRODUCTION

The Kamasutra is divided into seven books, each dealing with different aspects of sexual relationships and human behavior. The first book deals with general principles and introduces the concept of the four goals of life: dharma (duty), artha (wealth), kama (pleasure), and moksha (liberation). The second book discusses sexual attraction, courtship, and marriage, and emphasizes the importance of mutual consent and communication in relationships.

The third and fourth books focus on different sexual positions and techniques, including foreplay, oral sex, and various sexual positions. These books also include descriptions of various types of men and women and their sexual preferences.

The fifth and sixth books deal with adultery, prostitution, and other taboo topics. They also discuss sexual health and hygiene, contraception, and sexual satisfaction.

The seventh and final book talks about the art of seduction, ways to attract a partner, and the importance of being charming, humorous, and intelligent.

The Kamasutra is a unique work that provides insight into the social and cultural attitudes towards sex and relationships in ancient India. It emphasizes the importance of mutual respect, communication, and experimentation in sexual relationships and provides a comprehensive guide to sexual behavior and pleasure. However, it has also been criticized for promoting gender inequality, objectification of women, and endorsing practices that are considered immoral or illegal in modern times.

I

Orgins

The origins of the Kamasutra can be traced back to ancient India during the Gupta period, around the 3rd century CE. The author of the text, Vatsyayana, was a Brahmin scholar who lived in the region now known as Uttar Pradesh.

The Kamasutra was written during a time of great intellectual and cultural flourishing in ancient India, known as the Golden Age. It was a period of significant advancements in art, literature, science, and philosophy, and the Kamasutra reflects this context.

The text draws from a range of earlier Indian texts, including the Vedas, the Mahabharata, and the Arthashastra. It is also heavily influenced by the principles of Hinduism, particularly the idea of dharma, or moral duty, and the pursuit of artha, or material success.

The Kamasutra was originally written in Sanskrit, the classical language of ancient India. It was not widely known or translated until the 19th century when it was introduced to the West by Sir Richard Burton.

Let's explore the origins of the Kamasutra in detail:

Historical Context: The Kamasutra was written during the Gupta period, a time of significant cultural and intellectual advancement in ancient India. The Gupta Empire, which lasted from the 4th to 6th century CE, fostered an environment that promoted art, literature, philosophy, and social discourse.

Authorship: The author of the Kamasutra is believed to be Vatsyayana, although not much is known about him. Vatsyayana remains an enigmatic figure, with little historical information available about his life and identity. Speculations and theories surround his background, but concrete details are scarce.

Influences and Sources: The Kamasutra drew inspiration from earlier Indian texts and traditions. It incorporated ideas from various fields, including literature, philosophy, and the arts. Some of the influences on the Kamasutra include the Arthashastra (an ancient treatise on governance and economics) and earlier works on love and relationships.

Purpose and Intention: The Kamasutra was not solely intended as a guide to sexual positions but aimed to be a comprehensive manual on human relationships, love, and intimacy. It explored various aspects of sexual behavior, emotional connection, and the art of living a fulfilling life. The text sought to provide guidance on attaining pleasure, maintaining harmonious relationships, and achieving spiritual fulfillment.

Cultural and Social Significance: The Kamasutra reflects the cultural and social attitudes of ancient India. It acknowledges the importance of love, desire, and sexual pleasure in human life and emphasizes the value of mutual consent, respect, and communication in relationships. The text's teachings were intended for the educated elite, and it reflected the societal norms and expectations of the time.

Manuscripts and Translations: Over time, the Kamasutra has been preserved in various manuscripts, with different versions and variations. It was not widely known or translated until the 19th century when Sir Richard Burton's English translation brought it to a broader audience in the West. Since then, numerous translations and adaptations have been made, contributing to its global recognition.

The origins of the Kamasutra lie in the intellectual and cultural milieu of ancient India, particularly during the Gupta period. It represents an exploration of human sexuality, relationships, and the pursuit of pleasure. While its content may be focused on intimate matters, the text encompasses a broader understanding of human nature, emotions, and the complexities of human connections.

The author and his intention

The Kamasutra, attributed to the sage Vatsyayana, is a profound exploration of human sexuality, relationships, and the pursuit of pleasure. While information about Vatsyayana's life remains scarce, the text itself provides valuable insights into the author's intentions and objectives.

Vatsyayana's primary intention in writing the Kamasutra was to create a comprehensive manual that would serve as a guide to navigating the complexities of love, desire, and intimacy. His aim was to provide individuals with practical wisdom and insights into enhancing their sexual experiences, fostering meaningful connections, and leading fulfilling lives.

Going beyond a mere compilation of sexual positions, the Kamasutra delves into the broader aspects of human nature, emotions, and the dynamics of relationships. Vatsyayana recognized that sexual pleasure is intricately intertwined with emotional, intellectual, and spiritual dimensions. He believed that by understanding and embracing the various facets of our human desires, we can cultivate deeper connections with ourselves and our partners.

In addition to the physical aspects of sexual pleasure, the Kamasutra addresses the importance of consent, communication, and mutual respect in relationships. Vatsyayana recognized that open dialogue and understanding between partners are vital for creating an environment of trust and intimacy. His teachings emphasized the significance of active participation, exploration, and the willingness to fulfill one another's needs and desires.

The Kamasutra also reflects the cultural and social attitudes of ancient India. It acknowledges the diversity of human desires and relationships, while also recognizing the societal expectations and norms of the time. Vatsyayana's intention was to provide guidance within the context of the society in which he lived, offering advice that would enhance individuals' experiences while maintaining harmony within the existing social fabric.

Beyond its historical significance, the Kamasutra remains a relevant and influential text in the modern world. Its teachings continue to inspire discussions and explorations of human sexuality and relationships. By examining the depths of desire, pleasure, and emotional connection, the Kamasutra invites individuals to embrace their own unique desires, foster intimacy, and cultivate fulfilling relationships.

Through the centuries, the Kamasutra has transcended cultural boundaries and has been appreciated by readers around the world. It serves as a testament to Vatsyayana's profound understanding of human nature and his enduring desire to enlighten individuals about the intricacies of love, desire, and the pursuit of pleasure and fulfillment in life.

An overview of ancient Indian society, beliefs, and values

Ancient Indian society was characterized by a rich and diverse cultural landscape with a long history spanning thousands of years. The beliefs, values, and social structures of ancient India were deeply influenced by Hinduism, which played a central role in shaping the fabric of society.

Social Structure:

Ancient Indian society was divided into a hierarchical system known as the caste system. The four main varnas, or castes, were the Brahmins (priests and scholars), Kshatriyas (warriors and rulers), Vaishyas (merchants and farmers), and Shudras (laborers and servants). Beyond the caste system, there were various social groups and communities.

Spiritual Beliefs:

Hinduism was the predominant religion, and its beliefs and practices permeated all aspects of life. The fundamental concepts of Hinduism included dharma (moral duty), karma (law of cause and effect), and moksha (liberation from the cycle of rebirth).

Vedic Literature:

The ancient Indian scriptures, known as the Vedas, formed the foundation of religious and philosophical thought. They consisted of hymns, rituals, and philosophical treatises that provided guidance on moral and ethical conduct.

Philosophy and Schools of Thought:

Ancient India was home to various philosophical schools, such as Vedanta, Samkhya, Yoga, and Nyaya. These schools explored concepts of metaphysics, epistemology, ethics, and the nature of reality.

Arts and Literature:

Ancient India had a rich literary tradition, with works ranging from epic poems like the Mahabharata and the Ramayana to treatises on diverse subjects like medicine, mathematics, and grammar. Sanskrit was the primary language of intellectual and literary discourse.

Gender Roles and Family Life:

The social structure in ancient India placed a strong emphasis on familial and societal obligations. Gender roles were defined, with men typically occupying positions of authority and women being responsible for domestic and familial affairs. However, there were exceptions, and women played significant roles as scholars, poets, and rulers.

Education and Scholarship:

Education was highly valued in ancient Indian society, with centers of learning known as gurukuls, where students received instruction from gurus (teachers). Scholars engaged in the pursuit of knowledge in various fields, including philosophy, science, mathematics, astronomy, and the arts.

Ancient Indian society was a vibrant and complex tapestry, characterized by its spiritual and philosophical depth, social structure, and cultural expressions. It laid the foundation for the development of diverse intellectual, artistic, and scientific pursuits that continue to influence the world to this day.

Apart from the Kamasutra, India has a rich history of ancient texts and practices related to health and wellness, spirituality, and philosophy. Some of the most notable ones are:

Ayurveda: Ayurveda is an ancient system of medicine that originated in India over 5,000 years ago. The word Ayurveda is derived from the Sanskrit words "ayur," which means life, and "veda," which means knowledge. Ayurveda is based on the idea that good health is achieved by balancing the mind, body, and spirit.

Ayurveda emphasizes the use of natural remedies to prevent and treat illnesses. These remedies include herbs, minerals, and other natural substances, as well as lifestyle changes such as diet and exercise. Ayurvedic practitioners take into account a person's unique constitution or "dosha" when prescribing remedies, as each individual is believed to have a unique balance of the three doshas: Vata, Pitta, and Kapha.

Yoga: Yoga is a physical, mental, and spiritual practice that originated in ancient India. The word yoga is derived from the Sanskrit word "yuj," which means to unite or join. Yoga is based on the idea that the mind and body are interconnected, and that a healthy body is essential for a healthy mind.

Yoga involves various postures, breathing techniques, and meditation, which are believed to improve physical and mental health. The practice of yoga is also associated with stress reduction, improved flexibility, and increased strength.

Vedic literature: The Vedas are a collection of ancient Hindu texts that contain knowledge related to various fields, including philosophy, astronomy, and mathematics. The Vedas are considered the oldest scriptures in the world and are believed to have been composed between 1500 BCE and 500 BCE.

The Vedas contain knowledge related to the nature of reality, the purpose of life, and the principles of ethics and morality. They also contain information about rituals, sacrifices, and hymns. The four Vedas are Rigveda, Yajurveda, Samaveda, and Atharvaveda.

Jyotish: Jyotish is an ancient Indian system of astrology that is based on the position of celestial bodies at the time of a person's birth. The word Jyotish is derived from the Sanskrit word "jyoti," which means light.

Jyotish is believed to provide insights into a person's personality, relationships, and future. The system of Jyotish is based on the idea that the position of the planets and stars at the time of a person's birth can influence their life and destiny.

Meditation: Meditation is a practice that has been in existence in India for thousands of years. The word meditation is derived from the Latin word "meditatio," which means to think or contemplate.

Meditation involves the cultivation of a focused and calm mind, which is believed to reduce stress, anxiety, and improve overall well-being. There are many different forms of meditation, including mindfulness meditation, transcendental meditation, and loving-kindness meditation.

II

Vedic heritage

The earliest foundations of the kamasutra are found in the Vedic era literature of Hinduism.Vatsyayana acknowledges this heritage in verse 1.1.9 of the text where he names Svetaketu Uddalaka as the "first human author of the kamasutra". Uddalaka is an early Upanishadic rishi (scholar-poet, sage), whose ideas are found in the Brihadaranyaka Upanishad such as in section 6.2, and the Chandogya Upanishad such as over the verses 5.3 through 5.10. These Hindu scriptures are variously dated between 900 BCE and 700 BCE, according to the Indologist and Sanskrit scholar Patrick Olivelle. Among with other ideas such as Atman (self, soul) and the ontological concept of Brahman, these early Upanishads discuss human life, activities and the nature of existence as a form of internalized worship, where sexuality and sex is mapped into a form of religious yajna ritual (sacrificial fire, Agni) and suffused in spiritual terms:

A fire – that is what a woman is, Gautama.
Her firewood is the vulva,
her smoke is the pubic hair,
her flame is the vagina,
when one penetrates her, that is her embers,
and her sparks are the climax.
In that very fire the gods offer semen,

and from that offering springs a man.

– Brihadaranyaka Upanishad 6.2.13, 700 BCE, Trans.: Patrick Olivelle

According to the Indologist De, a view with which Doniger agrees, this is one of the many evidences that the kamasutra began in the religious literature of the Vedic era, ideas that were ultimately refined and distilled into a sutra-genre text by Vatsyayana.According to Doniger, this paradigm of celebrating pleasures, enjoyment and sexuality as a dharmic act began in the "earthy, vibrant text known as the Rigveda" of the Hindus. The Kamasutra and celebration of sex, eroticism and pleasure is an integral part of the religious milieu in Hinduism and quite prevalent in its temples.

Epics

Human relationships, sex and emotional fulfillment are a significant part of the post-Vedic Sanskrit literature such as the major Hindu epics: the Mahabharata and the Ramayana. The ancient Indian view has been, states Johann Meyer, that love and sex are a delightful necessity. Though she is reserved and selective, "a woman stands in very great need of suṛata (amorous or sexual pleasure)", and "the woman has a far stronger erotic disposition, her delight in the sexual act is greater than a man's".

Manuscripts

The Kamasutra manuscripts have survived in many versions across the Indian subcontinent. While attempting to get a translation of the Sanskrit kama-sastra text *Anangaranga* that had already been widely translated by the Hindus in regional languages such as Marathi, associates of the British Orientalist Richard Burton stumbled into portions of the Kamasutra manuscript. He commissioned the Sanskrit scholar Bhagvanlal Indraji to locate a complete Kamasutra manuscript and translate it. Indraji collected variant manuscripts in libraries and temples of Varanasi, Kolkata and Jaipur. Burton published an edited English translation of these manuscripts, but not a critical edition of the Kamasutra in Sanskrit.

According to S.C. Upadhyaya, known for his 1961 scholarly study and a more accurate translation of the Kamasutra, there are issues with the manuscripts that have survived and the text likely underwent revisions over time.This is confirmed by other 1st-millennium CE Hindu texts on kama that mention and cite the Kamasutra, but some of these quotations credited to the Kamasutra by these historic authors "are not to be found in the text of the Kamasutra" that have survived.

III

Contents

Vatsyayana's Kama Sutra states it has 1,250 verses distributed over 36 chapters in 64 sections organised into 7 books. This statement is included in the opening chapter of the text, a common practice in ancient Hindu texts likely included to prevent major and unauthorized expansions of a popular text. The text that has survived into the modern era has 67 sections, and this list is enumerated in Book 7 and in Yashodhara's Sanskrit commentary (bhasya) on the text.

The Kamasutra uses a mixture of prose and poetry, and the narration has the form of a dramatic fiction where two characters are called the nayaka (man) and nayika (woman), aided by the characters called pitamarda (libertine), vita (pander) and vidushaka (jester). This format follows the teachings found in the Sanskrit classic named the Natyasastra.The teachings and discussions found in the Kamasutra extensively incorporate ancient Hindu mythology and legends.

Kamasutra

Book. ChapterVerses ,Topics

1 . General remarks

1.1 1–24 Preface, history of kama literature, outline of the contents

1.2 1–40 Suitable age for kama knowledge, the three goals of life: dharma, Artha, Kama; their essential interrelationship, natural human questions

1.3 1–22 Preparations for kama, sixty four arts for a better quality of life, how girls can learn and train in these arts, their lifelong benefits and contribution to better kama

1.4 1–39 The life of an urban gentleman, work routine, entertainment and festivals, sports, picnics, socialization, games, entertainment and drinking parties, finding aids (messengers, friends, helpers) to improve success in kama, options for rural gentlemen, what one must never do in their pursuit of kama

1.5 1–37 Types of women, finding sexual partners, sex, being lovers, being faithful, permissible women, adultery and when to commit it, the forbidden women whom one must avoid, discretion with messengers and helpers, few dos and don't in life

2. Amorous advances/sexual union

2.1 1–45 Sexual relationships and the pleasure of sex, uniqueness of every lover, temperaments, sizes, endurance, foreplay, types of love and lovers, duration of sex, types of climax, intimacy, joy

2.2 1–31 Figuring out if someone is interested, conversations, prelude and preparation, touching each other, massage, embracing

2.3 –51–32, 1–31, 1–43 Kissing, where to kiss and how, teasing each other and games, signals and hints for the other person, cleanliness, taking care of teeth, hair, body, nails, physical non-sexual forms of intimacy (scratching, poking, biting, slapping, holding her)

2.6 –101–52 Intercourse, what it is and how, positions, various methods, bringing variety, usual and unusual sex, communicating before and during intercourse (moaning), diverse regional practices and customs, the needs of a man, the needs of a woman, variations and surprises, oral sex for women, oral sex for men, opinions, disagreements, experimenting with each other, the first time, why sexual excitement fades, reviving passion, quarreling, keeping sex exciting, sixty four methods to find happiness in a committed relationship

3. Acquiring a wife

3.1 1–24 Marriage, finding the right girl, which one to avoid, which one to persuade, how to decide, how to proceed, making alliances

3.2 –31–35, 1–32 Earning her trust, importance of not rushing things and being gentle, moving towards sexual openness gradually, how to approach a woman, proceeding to friendship, from friendship to intimacy, interpreting different responses of a girl

3.4 –51–55, 1–30 Earning his trust, knowing the man and his advances, how a woman can make advances, winning the heart; utilizing confidants of your lover, types of marriage, formalizing marriage, eloping

4. Duties and privileges of the wife

4.1 –21–48, 1–30 Being a wife, her life, conduct, power over the household, duties when her husband is away, nuclear and joint families, when to take charge and when not to

4.2 30–72 Remarriage, being unlucky, harems,[note 2] polygamy

5Other men's wives

5.1 1–56 Human nature, tendencies of men, tendencies of women, why women lose interest and start looking elsewhere, avoiding adultery, pursuing adultery, finding women interested in extramarital sex

5.2 –51–28, 1–28, 1–66, 1–37 Finding many lovers, deploying messengers, the need for them and how to find good go-betweens, getting acquainted, how to make a pass, gifts and love tokens, arranging meetings, how to discretely find out if a woman is available and interested, warnings and knowing when to stop

5.6 1–48 Public women [prostitution], their life, what to expect and not, how to find them, regional practices, guarding and respecting them

6. About courtesans

6.1 1–33 Courtesans, what motivates them, how to find clients, deciding if someone should just be a friend or a lover, which lovers to avoid, getting a lover and keeping him interested

6.2 1–76 How to please your lover

6.3 1–46 Making a lover go crazy about you, how to get rid of him if love life is not fulfilling

6.4 –51–43, 1–39 Methods to make an ex-lover interested in you again, reuniting, methods, checking if it is worth the effort, types of lovers, things to consider

6.6 1–53 Why love life gets dull, examples, familiarity and doubts

7 . Occult practices

7.1 –21–51, 1–51 Looking good, feeling good, why and how to be attractive, bewitching, being virile, paying attention, genuineness and artificiality, body art and perforations, taking care of one's sexual organs, stimulants, prescriptions and unusual practices.

On Balance in life

In any period of life in which
one of the elements of the trivarga
– dharma, artha, kama –
is the primary one, the other two
should be natural adjuncts of it.
Under no circumstances, should any one of the
trivarga be detrimental to the other two.

—Kamasutra 1.2.1,
Translator: Ludo Rocher

IV

Kamasutra

Across human cultures, states Michel Foucault, "the truth of sex" has been produced and shared by two processes. One method has been ars erotica texts, while the other has been the scientia sexualis literature. The first are typically of the hidden variety and shared by one person to another, between friends or from a master to a student, focusing on the emotions and experience, sans physiology. These bury many of the truths about sex and human sexual nature.The second are empirical studies of the type found in biology, physiology and medical texts, focusing on the physiology and objective observations, sans emotions.The Kamasutra belongs to both camps, states Doniger. It discusses, in its distilled form, the physiology, the emotions and the experience while citing and quoting prior Sanskrit scholarship on the nature of kama.

The Kamasutra is a "sutra"-genre text consisting of intensely condensed, aphoristic verses. Doniger describes them as a "kind of atomic string (thread) of meanings", which are so cryptic that any translation is more like deciphering and filling in the text.Condensing a text into a sutra-genre religious text form makes it easier to remember and transmit, but it also introduces ambiguity and the need to understand the context of each chapter, its philological roots, as well as the prior literature, states Doniger.However, this method of knowledge preservation and transmission has its foundation in the Vedas, which themselves are cryptic and require a commentator and teacher-guide to comprehend the details and the inter-relationship of the ideas.The Kamasutra too has attracted commentaries, of which the most well known are those of 12th-century or 13th-century Yaśodhara's Jayamaṅgalā in the Sanskrit language, and of Devadatta Shastri who commented on the original text as well as its commentaries in the Hindi language. There are many other Sanskrit commentaries on the Kamasutra, such as the Sutra Vritti by Narsingha Sastri.These commentaries on the Kamasutra cite and quote text from other Hindu texts such as the Upanishads, the Arthashastra, the Natyashastra, the Manusmriti, the Nyayasutra, the Markandeya Purana, the Mahabharata, the Nitishastra and others to provide the context, per the norms of its literary traditions.The extant translations of the Kamasutra typically incorporate these commentaries, states Daniélou.

In the colonial era marked by sexual censorship, the Kamasutra became famous as a pirated and underground text for its explicit description of sex positions. The stereotypical image of the text is one where erotic pursuit with sexual intercourse include improbable contortionist forms. In reality, according to Doniger, the real Kamasutra is much more and is a book about "the art of living", about understanding one's body and a partner's body, finding a partner and emotional connection, marriage, the power equation over time in intimate relationships, the nature of adultery and drugs (aphrodisiacs) along with many simple to complex variations in sex positions to explore. It is also a psychological treatise that presents the effect of desire and pleasure on human behavior.

For each aspect of Kama, the Kamasutra presents a diverse spectrum of options and regional practices. According to Shastri, as quoted by Doniger, the text analyses "the inclinations of men, good and bad", thereafter it presents Vatsyayana's recommendation and arguments of what one must avoid as well as what to not miss in experiencing and enjoying, with "acting only on the good".For example, the text discusses adultery but recommends a faithful spousal relationship.The approach of Kamasutra is not to ignore nor deny the psychology and complexity of human behavior for pleasure and sex. The text, according to Doniger, clearly states "that a treatise demands the inclusion of everything, good or bad", but after being informed with in-depth knowledge, one must "reflect and accept only the good". The approach found in the text is one where goals of science and religion should not be to repress, but to encyclopedically know and understand, thereafter let the individual make the choice.The text states that it aims to be comprehensive and inclusive of diverse views and lifestyles.

Flirting and courtship

The 3rd-century text includes a number of themes, including subjects such as flirting that resonate in the modern era context, states a New York Times review. For example, it suggests that a young man seeking to attract a woman, should hold a party, and invite the guests to recite poetry. In the party, a poem should be read with parts missing, and the guests should compete to creatively complete the poem. As another example, the Kamasutra suggests that the boy and the girl should go play together, such as swim in a river. The boy should dive into the water away from the girl he is interested in, then swim underwater to get close to her, emerge from the water and surprise her, touch her slightly and then dive again, away from her.

Book 3 of the Kamasutra is largely dedicated to the art of courtship with the aim of marriage. The book's opening verse declares marriage to be a conducive means to "a pure and natural love between the partners", states Upadhyaya.It leads to emotional fulfillment in many forms such as more friends for both, relatives, progeny, amorous and sexual relationship between the couple, and the conjugal pursuit of *dharma* (spiritual and ethical life) and artha (economic life).The first three chapters discuss how a man should go about finding the right bride, while the fourth offers equivalent discussion for a woman and how she can get the man she wants.The text states that a person should be realistic, and must possess the "same qualities which one expects from the partner". It suggests involving one's friends and relatives in the search, and meeting the current friends and relatives of one's future partner prior to the marriage.While the original text makes no mention of astrology and horoscopes, later commentaries on the Kamasutra such as one by 13th-century Yashodhara includes consulting and comparing the compatibility of the horoscopes, omens, planetary alignments, and such signs prior to proposing a marriage. Vatsyayana recommends, states Alain Danielou, that "one should play, marry, associate with one's equals, people of one's own circle" who share the same values and religious outlook. It is more difficult to manage a good, happy relationship when there are basic differences between the two, according to verse 3.1.20 of the Kamasutra.

Intimacy and foreplay

Vatsyayana's Kamasutra describes intimacy of various forms, including those between lovers before and during sex. For example, the text discusses eight forms of *alingana* (embrace) in verses 2.2.7–23: *sphrishtaka, viddhaka, udghrishtaka, piditaka, lataveshtitaka, vrikshadhirudha, tilatandula and kshiranira.* The first four are expressive of mutual love, but are nonsexual. The last four are forms of embrace recommended by Vatsyayana to increase pleasure during foreplay and during sexual intimacy. Vatsyayana cites earlier – now lost – Indian texts from the Babhraya's school, for these eight categories of embraces. The various forms of intimacy reflect the intent and provide means to engage a combination of senses for pleasure. For instance, according to Vatsyayana the lalatika form enables both to feel each other and allows the man to visually appreciate "the full beauty of the female form", states S.C. Upadhyaya.

On sexual embraces

Some sexual embraces, not in this text,
also intensify passion;
these, too, may be used for love-making,
but only with care.
The territory of the text extends
only so far as men have dull appetites;
but when the wheel of sexual ecstasy is in full motion,
there is no textbook at all, and no order.

—Kamasutra 2.2.30–31,
Translator: Wendy Doniger and Sudhir Kakar

Another example of the forms of intimacy discussed in the Kamasutra includes chumbanas (kissing).The text presents twenty-six forms of kisses, ranging from those appropriate for showing respect and affection, to those during foreplay and sex. Vatsyayana also mentions variations in kissing cultures in different parts of ancient India. The best kiss for an intimate partner, according to kamasutra, is one that is based on the awareness of the avastha (the emotional state of one's partner) when the two are not in a sexual union. During sex, the text recommends going with the flow and mirroring with *abhiyoga* and *samprayoga.*

Other techniques of foreplay and sexual intimacy described in the kamasutra include various forms of holding and embraces *(grahana, upaguhana)*, mutual massage and rubbing *(mardana)*, pinching and biting, using fingers and hands to stimulate *(karikarakrida, nadi-kshobana, anguli-pravesha)*, three styles of jihva-pravesha (french kissing), and many styles of fellatio and cunnlingus.

Adultery

The Kamasutra, states the Indologist and Sanskrit literature scholar Ludo Rocher, discourages adultery but then devotes "not less than fifteen sutras (1.5.6–20) to enumerating the reasons (karana) for which a man is allowed to seduce a married woman". Vatsyayana mentions different types of nayikas (urban girls) such as unmarried virgins, those married and abandoned by husband, widow seeking remarriage and courtesans, then discusses their kama/sexual education, rights and mores. In childhood, Vātsyāyana says, a person should learn how to make a living; youth is the time for pleasure, and as years pass, one should concentrate on living virtuously and hope to escape the cycle of rebirth.

According to Doniger, the Kamasutra teaches adulterous sexual liaison as a means for a man to predispose the involved woman in assisting him, as a strategic means to work against his enemies and to facilitate his successes. It also explains the signs and reasons a woman wants to enter into an adulterous relationship and when she does not want to commit adultery.The Kamasutra teaches strategies to engage in adulterous relationships, but concludes its chapter on sexual liaison stating that one should not commit adultery because adultery pleases only one of two sides in a marriage, hurts the other, it goes against both *dharma* and *artha.*

Caste and Class

The Kamasutra has been one of the unique sources of sociological information and cultural milieu of ancient India. It shows a "near total disregard of class (varna) and caste (jati)", states Doniger. Human relationships, including the sexual type, are neither segregated nor repressed by gender or caste, rather linked to individual's wealth (success in artha). In the pages of the Kamasutra, lovers are "not upper-class" but they "must be rich" enough to dress well, pursue social leisure activities, buy gifts and surprise the lover. In the rare mention of caste found in the text, it is about a man finding his legal wife and the advice that humorous stories to seduce a woman should be about "other virgins of same jati (caste)". In general, the text describes sexual activity between men and women across class and caste, both in urban and rural settings.

Same-sex relationships

The Kamasutra includes verses describing homosexual relations such as oral sex between two men, as well as between two women. Lesbian relations are extensively covered in Chapters 5 and 8 in Book 2 of the text.

According to Doniger, the Kamasutra discusses same-sex relationships through the notion of the tritiya prakriti, literally, "third sexuality" or "third nature". In Redeeming the Kamasutra, Doniger states that "the Kamasutra departs from the dharmic view of homosexuality in significant ways", where the term kliba appears. In contemporary translations, this has been inaccurately rendered as "eunuch" – or, a castrated man in a harem, and the royal harem did not exist in India before the Turkish presence in the ninth century. The Sanskrit word Kliba found in older Indian texts refers to a "man who does not act like a man", typically in a pejorative sense. The Kamasutra does not use the pejorative term kliba at all, but speaks instead of a "third nature" or, in the sexual behavior context as the "third sexuality".

The text states that there are two sorts of "third nature", one where a man behaves like a woman, and in the other, a woman behaves like a man. In one of the longest consecutive sets of verses describing a sexual act, the Kamasutra describes fellatio technique between a man dressed like a woman performing fellatio on another man.The text also mentions same-sex behavior between two women, such as a girl losing her virginity with a girlfriend as they use their fingers,as well as oral sex and the use of sex toys between women. Svairini, a term Danielou translates as a lesbian,is described in the text as a woman who lives a conjugal life with another woman or by herself fending for herself, not interested in a husband. Additionally, the text has some fleeting remarks on bisexual relationships.

The Kamasutra also mentions "pretend play" sadomasochism, and group sex.

V

Translations

According to Doniger, the historical records suggest that the Kamasutra was a well-known and popular text in Indian history. This popularity through the Mughal Empire era is confirmed by its regional translations. The Mughals, states Doniger, had "commissioned lavishly illustrated Persian and Sanskrit *Kamasutra* manuscripts".

The first English translation of the Kama Sutra was privately printed in 1883 by the Orientalist Sir Richard Francis Burton. He did not translate it, but did edit it to suit the Victorian British attitudes. The unedited translation was produced by the Indian scholar Bhagwan Lal Indraji with the assistance of a student Shivaram Parshuram Bhide, under the guidance of Burton's friend, the Indian civil servant Forster Fitzgerald Arbuthnot. According to Doniger, the Burton version is a "flawed English translation" but influential as modern translators and abridged versions of Kamasutra even in the Indian languages such as Hindi are re-translations of the Burton version, rather than the original Sanskrit manuscript.

The Burton version of the Kamasutra was produced in an environment where Victorian mindset and Protestant proselytizers were busy finding faults and attacking Hinduism and its culture, rejecting as "filthy paganism" anything sensuous and sexual in Hindu arts and literature. The "Hindus were cowering under their scorn", states Doniger, and the open discussion of sex in the Kamasutra scandalized the 19th-century Europeans.The Burton edition of the Kamasutra was illegal to publish in England and the United States till 1962. Yet, states Doniger, it became soon after its publication in 1883, "one of the most pirated books in the English language", widely copied, reprinted and republished sometimes without Richard Burton's name.

Burton made two important contributions to the Kamasutra. First, he had the courage to publish it in the colonial era against the political and cultural mores of the British elite. He creatively found a way to subvert the then prevalent censorship laws of Britain under the Obscene Publications Act of 1857. Burton created a fake publishing house named *The Kama Shastra Society of London and Benares* (Benares = Varanasi), with the declaration that it is "for private circulation only".The second major contribution was to edit it in a major way, by changing words and rewriting sections to make it more acceptable to the general British public. For example, the original Sanskrit Kamasutra does not use the words lingam or yoni for sexual organs, and almost always uses other terms. Burton adroitly avoided being viewed as obscene to the Victorian mindset by avoiding the use of words such as penis, vulva, vagina and other direct or indirect sexual terms in the Sanskrit text to discuss sex, sexual relationships and human sexual positions. Burton used the terms lingam and yoni instead throughout the translation. This conscious and incorrect word substitution, states Doniger, thus served as an Orientalist means to "anthropologize sex, distance it, make it safe for English readers by assuring them, or pretending to assure them, that the text was not about real sexual organs, their sexual organs, but merely about the appendages of weird, dark people far away." Though Burton used the terms lingam and yoni for human sexual organs, terms that actually mean a lot more in Sanskrit texts and its meaning depends on the context. However, Burton's Kamasutra gave a unique, specific meaning to these words in the western imagination.

The problems with Burton mistranslation are many, states Doniger. First, the text "simply does not say what Burton says it says". Second, it "robs women of their voices, turning direct quotes into indirect quotes, thus losing the force of the dialogue that animates the work and erasing the vivid presence of the many women who speak in the Kamasutra". Third, it changes the force of words in the original text. For example, when a woman says "Stop!" or "Let me go!" in the original text of Vatsyayana, Burton changed it to "She continually utters words expressive of prohibition, sufficiency, or desire of liberation", states Doniger, and thus misconstrues the context and intent of the original text. Similarly, while the original Kamasutra acknowledges that "women have strong privileges", Burton erased these passages and thus eroded women's agency in ancient India in the typical Orientialist manner that dehumanized the Indian culture. David Shulman, a professor of Indian Studies and Comparative Religion, agrees with Doniger that the Burton translation is misguided and flawed. The Burton version was written with a different mindset, one that treated "sexual matters with Victorian squeamishness and a pornographic delight in the indirect", according to Shulman. It has led to a misunderstanding of the text and created the wrong impression of it being ancient "Hindu pornography".

In 1961, S. C. Upadhyaya published his translation as the Kamasutra of Vatsyayana: Complete Translation from the Original. According to Jyoti Puri, it is considered among the best-known scholarly English-language translations of the Kamasutra in post-independent India.

Other translations include those by Alain Daniélou (The Complete Kama Sutra in 1994). This translation, originally into French, and thence into English, featured the original text attributed to Vatsyayana, along with a medieval and a modern commentary. Unlike the 1883 version, Daniélou's new translation preserves the numbered verse divisions of the original, and does not incorporate notes in the text. He includes English translations of two important commentaries, one by Jayamangala, and a more modern commentary by Devadatta Shastri, as endnotes. Doniger questions the accuracy of Daniélou's translation, stating that he has freely reinterpreted the Kamasutra while disregarding the gender that is implicit in the Sanskrit words. He, at times, reverses the object and subject, making the woman the subject and man the object when the Kamasutra is explicitly stating the reverse. According to Doniger, "even this cryptic text [Kamasutra] is not infinitely elastic" and such creative reinterpretations do not reflect the text.

A translation by Indra Sinha was published in 1980. In the early 1990s, its chapter on sexual positions began circulating on the Internet as an independent text and today is often assumed to be the whole of the Kama Sutra.

Doniger and Sudhir Kakar published another translation in 2002, as a part of the Oxford World's Classics series. Along with the translation, Doniger has published numerous articles and book chapters relating to the Kamasutra. The Doniger translation and Kamasutra-related literature has both been praised and criticized. According to David Shulman, the Doniger translation "will change peoples' understanding of this book and of ancient India. Previous translations are hopelessly outdated, inadequate and misguided". Narasingha Sil calls the Doniger's work as "another signature work of translation and exegesis of the much misunderstood and abused Hindu erotology". Her translation has the folksy, "twinkle prose", engaging style, and an original translation of the Sanskrit text. However, adds Sil, Doniger's work mixes her postmodern translation and interpretation of the text with her own "political and polemical" views. She makes sweeping generalizations and flippant insertions that are supported by neither the original text nor the weight of evidence in other related ancient and later Indian literature such as from the Bengal Renaissance movement – one of the scholarly specialty of Narasingha Sil. Doniger's presentation style titillates, yet some details misinform and parts of her interpretations are dubious, states Sil.

VI

Legacy of Kamasutra in the Modern World

The legacy of the Kamasutra in the modern world is multi-faceted and far-reaching. Here are some aspects that highlight its enduring influence:

Cultural and Artistic Impact: The Kamasutra has left an indelible mark on global culture and the arts. Its depictions of human sensuality and sexual expression have inspired artists, writers, filmmakers, and performers. It has influenced various art forms, including paintings, sculptures, literature, dance, and theater, contributing to the celebration of human sexuality as a subject of artistic exploration.

Popular Perception and Stereotypes: The Kamasutra has contributed to popular perceptions and stereotypes about Indian sexuality. It is often associated with exoticism and the notion of an ancient, sexually liberated India. While these stereotypes can be oversimplified and distorted, they reflect the enduring fascination and intrigue surrounding the text.

Influence on Modern Sexuality: The Kamasutra has played a role in shaping modern perceptions of human sexuality. It has contributed to discussions on sexual liberation, individual desires, and diverse sexual practices. The text's teachings on communication, consent, and sexual pleasure have influenced modern approaches to healthy and fulfilling sexual relationships.

Inspiration for Sex Education: The Kamasutra has provided inspiration and reference material for contemporary sex education. While modern sex education focuses on comprehensive and evidence-based approaches, the Kamasutra's teachings have contributed to broader discussions on sexual well-being, pleasure, and the importance of consent and communication.

Exploration of Intimacy and Relationships: The Kamasutra's exploration of emotional intimacy, mutual respect, and the art of building fulfilling relationships continues to be relevant in the modern world. It has encouraged individuals and couples to explore deeper connections, understand their desires, and foster meaningful relationships based on trust, communication, and consent.

Academic and Scholarly Research: The Kamasutra has been a subject of scholarly research, providing insights into ancient Indian culture, societal norms, and sexual practices. Academics, historians, and anthropologists continue to study the text, contributing to a better understanding of ancient Indian society and its attitudes towards sexuality.

Empowerment and Agency: The Kamasutra, with its emphasis on pleasure, consent, and sexual agency, has contributed to discussions on sexual empowerment. It has encouraged individuals to embrace their desires, communicate their needs, and make informed choices in their sexual lives.

Critique and Controversies: The Kamasutra has faced criticism and controversies for various reasons, including its historical context, cultural interpretations, and potential misrepresentations. Some argue that it perpetuates patriarchal norms and objectification of women. These debates have led to critical examinations of the text, contributing to broader discussions on consent, gender equality, and sexual ethics.

The legacy of the Kamasutra in the modern world is complex and multifaceted. While it has faced both acclaim and criticism, its enduring influence on popular culture, art, sexuality discourse, and scholarly research demonstrates its significance as a historical and cultural landmark.

Impact

The Kamasutra has imparted valuable lessons and had a transformative impact on the world. Here's an in-depth exploration of what we can learn from the Kamasutra and how it has changed the world:

Embracing Sexual Diversity: The Kamasutra teaches us to appreciate and embrace the diversity of human sexuality. It acknowledges that desires and preferences vary among individuals and encourages a non-judgmental attitude towards different expressions of intimacy and pleasure. By recognizing and respecting sexual diversity, the Kamasutra has played a part in fostering a more inclusive and accepting world.

Communication and Consent: One of the key lessons from the Kamasutra is the importance of open communication and mutual consent in sexual relationships. It emphasizes the significance of understanding and expressing one's desires and boundaries while respecting those of their partner. By promoting healthy communication and consent, the Kamasutra has contributed to the establishment of more respectful and consensual sexual encounters.

Intimacy Beyond Physicality: The Kamasutra goes beyond the physical aspects of sex and highlights the significance of emotional and intellectual intimacy. It teaches us that a fulfilling sexual relationship is not solely based on physical pleasure but requires a deep connection, understanding, and shared experiences. By emphasizing the holistic nature of intimacy, the Kamasutra has broadened our perspectives on what constitutes a satisfying sexual relationship.

Mutual Pleasure and Satisfaction: The Kamasutra places importance on mutual pleasure and satisfaction in sexual encounters. It encourages partners to focus on the pleasure of their companion and highlights the reciprocal nature of intimacy. This emphasis on mutual pleasure has helped shift the narrative around sexuality from a solely self-centered experience to a shared journey of pleasure and fulfillment.

Empowering Sexual Agency: The Kamasutra empowers individuals to embrace and assert their sexual agency. It encourages self-exploration and understanding of one's desires, providing a framework for individuals to make informed choices about their sexual lives. By promoting sexual agency, the Kamasutra has played a role in empowering individuals to take ownership of their sexuality and make decisions that align with their values and preferences.

Historical and Cultural Insights: Studying the Kamasutra offers us a window into the historical and cultural context of ancient India. It provides valuable insights into the societal attitudes, values, and practices of that time, allowing us to appreciate the rich cultural heritage of India. By understanding the historical roots of the Kamasutra, we gain a deeper appreciation for the diversity and evolution of human sexuality across different cultures and time periods.

The Kamasutra has changed the world by challenging societal taboos surrounding sexuality, fostering open discussions, and promoting a more nuanced understanding of human desire and relationships. It has inspired scholars, artists, and individuals to explore and celebrate the complexity of human sexuality. By encouraging open-mindedness, communication, and respect, the Kamasutra has contributed to the creation of a more inclusive and empowering sexual culture.

9 798890 265852

Printed by Libri Plureos GmbH in Hamburg,
Germany